For Douglas
GM

For Anna, Mika and Kaia
SMK

The Duck and the Darklings

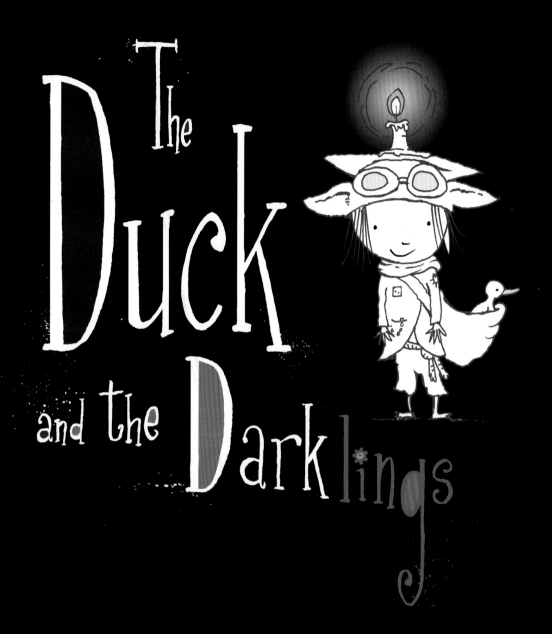

Glenda Millard

Stephen Michael King

ALLEN&UNWIN

SYDNEY·MELBOURNE·AUCKLAND·LONDON

In the land of Dark

grew a child

called

Peterboy.

Home was a hole
built with care,
lit with love,

where he

and Grandpapa

shared everything.

Dark

was a
sorry,
spoiled place;
a **broken** and
battered place.

It had been that way
for so long that **sunups**
and **sundowns,**
yesterdays and tomorrows
and almost everything
in them had been
disremembered
by each and by all . . .

except **Grandpapa.**

The old ones never
brightened their gloomy
burrows with tales of
the long-ago, when all
was bright and beautiful.

They dared not look at
their ruined world.

Only when the heavenlies were deepest indigo and earth was darkest violet were Peterboy and the other Darkling childs sent up and out to the finding fields.

Over heaps and hummocks of lost and lonely things they clambered, gathering fiddlesticks for firewood, filling billies with trickle and seeking crumbs and crusts of comfort to take home.

When he returned to Grandpapa,
Peterboy painted word pictures of
the mysteries he had seen outside.

'There are holes
in the dark,
Grandpapa,
and light leaks
through!

It slides down the
steeps,
puddles in the deeps
and

glimmers on the
trickle.'

While Peterboy talked,

he saw light as dazzling as a falling

star in Grandpapa's eyes.

When he asked what it was,

the old man answered,

'Memories of things past,

child, **thoughts of things**

lost and longed for.'

The light
put longing into Peterboy's
heart.

When he returned to the finding fields,

his spiderling fingers

crept into cracks
and
crevices, corners
and
crannies.

He wished for more than crumbs and crusts.

He wished for a
scrap of wonderfulness.

Something

to bring light

to Grandpapa's eyes

and

keep

it there.

Instead

Peterboy found **Idaduck**.

He put his ear to the **downy heart**
of her and heard **hope** beating there,

and although he knew Grandpapa

would **grumble**,

Peterboy laid the broken duck

gently in his glory bag

and carried her home.

'There's little enough
to eat without feeding
someone else's child,'
said Grandpapa gruffly.

'Please let her stay,' begged Peterboy.

'She can share with me.'

'Only until she's cured then,' said Grandpapa.
'But don't get too fond of her; ducks are born
with wanderlust in them. They live for the
feel of wind in their wings.'

So **Idaduck** stayed.

With **cobwebs** and **cotton reels**,

tenderness

and

thistledown,

Grandpapa darned and cobbled until the **duck** was **mended from** top to tail;

quack,

waddle

and **wing**.

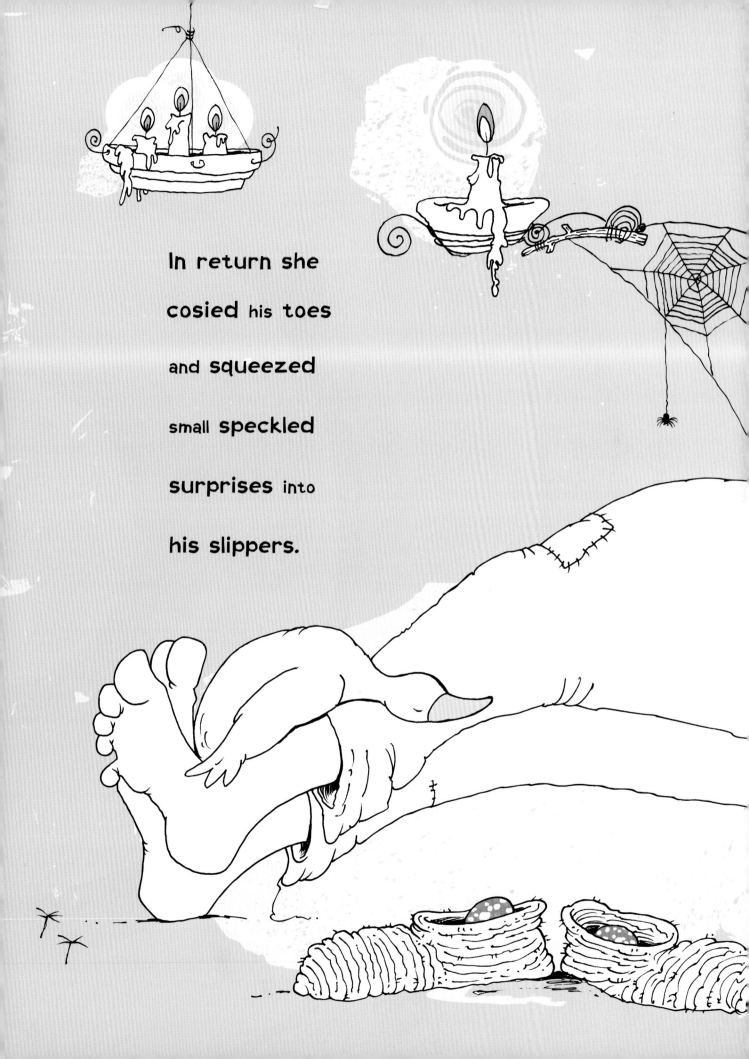

In return she
cosied his toes
and squeezed
small speckled
surprises into
his slippers.

Sometimes she and Peterboy
danced in the firelight
while Grandpapa played oompapas
on his curly brass tootle.
Other times when Peterboy
returned from the finding fields,
he would find Grandpapa nursing Idaduck,
his eyes a-glimmer and aglow
with forbidden fondness.

Peterboy couldn't remember
a time when Grandpapa was happier.

But the earth turned, the air cooled and wistful was the look in Idaduck's eyes. Peterboy remembered Grandpapa's warning about wanderlust and the wind. Worried by the great emptiness that would be left by a duck so small, Peterboy said,

'We must give Idaduck something that will make her want to stay.'

'We've given all that is ours to give,' answered Grandpapa.

'It isn't enough,' said Peterboy. 'Tell her about the long-ago, Grandpapa.'

'What good is there in telling tales of lost and longed-for things?' the old man asked.

'When you think about the long-ago, I see starlight in your eyes,' said Peterboy. 'Please, Grandpapa, fill our darkness with light, warm our wintery hearts with your stories.'

So Grandpapa turned the rusty latchkey of his magnificent remembery and set free a symphony of stories.

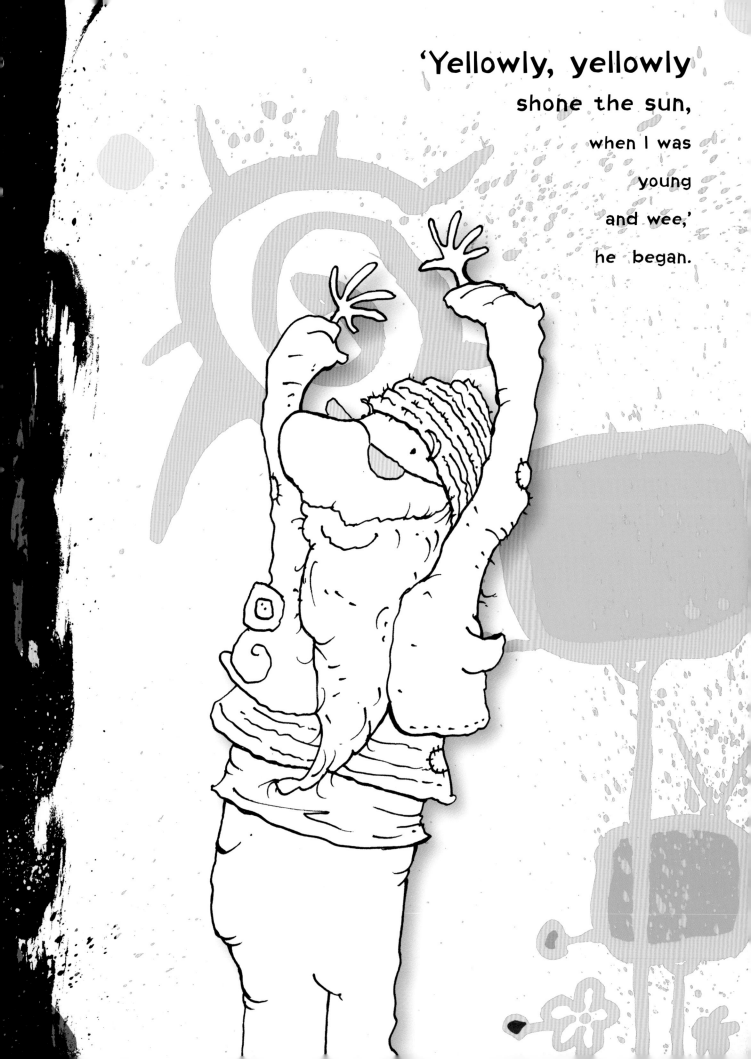

'Yellowly, yellowly
shone the sun,
when I was
young
and wee,'
he began.

Peterboy listened, his mind awash
with bright imaginings
as Grandpapa's shining,
shimmering words
painted windows on the walls.
He told of rainbows and rivers,
fields and flowers and trees
in tens of thousands.

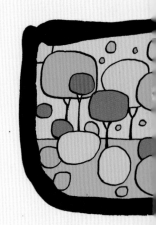

'Greenly, greenly breathed the forests,'
he said, 'and sweetly ripened the fruit.
Merrily winged the birdlets through
the periwinkle sky and daisily,
daisily bloomed the fields
                    where children played in peace.'

Grandpapa knew many
tales and when at last
they all were told,
he and the boy and
the duck dozed.

But the **wind**
whispered Idaduck's name
and she woke
and waddled
upstairs.

When Peterboy woke
he too climbed the stairs
and sat beside Idaduck.

Sorrydrops

fell

from

their

eyes.

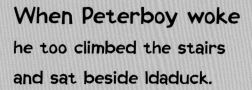

The sky was darkest indigo.

The earth was deepest violet

and the wind was soft as velvet.

But there was no star,

no fingernail

of mOOn

to light the way

for Idaduck.

Grandpapa woke and saw the boy and the duck.

And because he knew almost all there was to know, even the longings of the duck and the kindness of the boy, he said,

'Wait, Peterboy! You must give the duck such a fare-thee-well that it will never be disremembered. So fine and fitting that when people speak of it the stars will shine.'

So **Peterboy** lit his **candle-hat** and fetched his friends, the children of Dark. He told them about Idaduck, about the wanderlust and the velvet wind.

'Tell your old ones about the fine and fitting fare-thee-well. Ask them to come with us and to wear candle-hats,' he said.

'We must shine a great light to show Idaduck the way.'

Peterboy led the Darklings,

young and old,

to a clearing where they shared

crumbs of tenderness,

crusts of love

and small speckled surprises.

After they had eaten, the children of
Dark climbed a towering tree and sat upon
its needled boughs, their candle-hats ablaze
with light. Far below, Grandpapa
blew oompapas on his curly brass tootle and
the old ones danced and sang.

Courage gave Peterboy a voice.

He cried out from his lofty perch.

'One day I found a scrap of wonderfulness. Her wings were wounded but in her heart there was hope.

So I took her home.

Idaduck made stars shine in Grandpapa's eyes. But now she is mended and

we must say goodbye.'

The Darklings stood still. They had danced night to its end. The candles on their hats had burnt down to wicks and wax but all around them earth remained strangely bright and beautiful.

The old ones looked in shame for the wounds man had made. But time had soothed earth's hurts. She was dressed anew in flowers and forests.

The velvet wind whispered.
Idaduck spread her wings and the
Darklings watched with hope in their hearts

as she flew out of sight.

Glenda Millard is the author of many acclaimed picture books and novels, including *Lightning Jack* (with Patricia Mullins) and *For All Creatures* (with Rebecca Cool). **Stephen Michael King** has illustrated, written and designed many splendid books for children, including *A Bear and a Tree* and *Bella's Bad Hair Day*. The books they have made together include *Applesauce and the Christmas Miracle,* and *The Tender Moments of Saffron Silk* and other books in the Kingdom of Silk series.

First published in 2014

Allen & Unwin
83 Alexander Street
Crows Nest NSW 2065
Australia
Phone: (61 2) 8425 0100
Email: info@allenandunwin.com
Web: www.allenandunwin.com

A Cataloguing-in-Publication entry is available from the National Library of Australia
www.trove.nla.gov.au

ISBN 978 174331 261 2

Stephen Michael King created these illustrations using pen, brush, ink and digital compilation.

Cover and text design by STINGart
Set in Skizzors and Day Roman by STINGart
This book was printed in December 2013 by C & C Offset Printing Co., Ltd., C & C Building, Chunhu Industrial Estate, Pinghu, Longgang, Shenzhen, Guangdong, PRC, Post Code: 518111.

1 2 3 4 5 6 7 8 9 10